ARNIE
and the Stolen Markers

NANCY CARLSON

PUFFIN BOOKS

RS   PUFFIN BOOKS
Published by the Penguin Group
Viking Penguin, a division of Penguin Books USA Inc.,
40 West 23rd Street, New York, New York 10010, U.S.A.
Penguin Books Ltd, 27 Wrights Lane, London W8 5TZ, England
Penguin Books Australia Ltd, Ringwood, Victoria, Australia
Penguin Books Canada Ltd, 2801 John Street, Markham, Ontario, Canada L3R 1B4
Penguin Books (N.Z.) Ltd, 182–190 Wairau Road, Auckland 10, New Zealand

Penguin Books Ltd, Registered Offices: Harmondsworth, Middlesex, England

First published in the United States of America by Viking Penguin,
a division of Penguin Books USA Inc., 1987
Published in Picture Puffins 1989
1   3   5   7   9   10   8   6   4   2
Copyright © Nancy Carlson, 1987
All rights reserved

LIBRARY OF CONGRESS CATALOGING-IN-PUBLICATION DATA
Carlson, Nancy L.
Arnie and the stolen markers/by Nancy Carlson.   p.   cm.
Summary: After spending his allowance at Harvey's Toy Shop, Arnie
steals a set of markers and suffers the consequences of his action.
ISBN 0 14 050707 8
[1. Stealing—Fiction.   2. Honesty—Fiction.]   I. Title.
PZ7.C21665Ar   1989   [E]—dc19   89-30227

Printed in Japan by Dai Nippon Printing Co. Ltd.
Set in Clarendon Light

To the Andersons.
"Remember Saturday mornings
at Harvey's?"

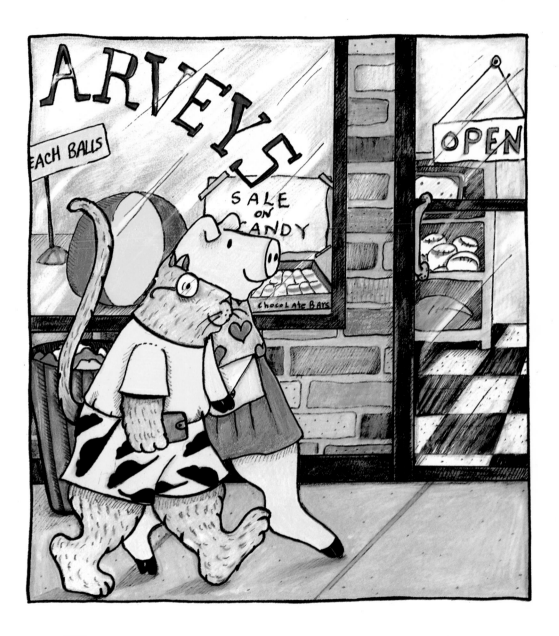

Every Saturday morning Arnie and Louanne
went to Harvey's Candy and Toy Shop.

Arnie always spent all his allowance on candy.
But Louanne would pick out neat toys and
save her allowance until she had enough
money to buy them.

One Saturday, after Arnie had spent every
penny on candy, he saw something
wonderful!!!

A super-duper marker set, with twenty
different colors.

Arnie had to have it!!

He asked Louanne if he could borrow
five dollars.
"No way! I'm saving for a new football,"
said Louanne.

"Boy, is she stingy," grumbled Arnie. "I must have this set. I could really have fun with it!"

"Hey, Arnie, let's go play!" said Louanne.

But Arnie decided to hang around Harvey's.
"I really, really need these markers,"
he thought.

Suddenly Arnie saw Harvey go into the
back room.

Without thinking, Arnie hid the marker set under his shirt and ran out the door.

As Arnie ran down the street he bumped right into Ms. Hoozit.

"Oops," said Arnie.

"Well, how are you, Arnie?" asked Ms. Hoozit.

"J-J-Just fine," said Arnie, and off he ran.

Arnie kept running until he got to his room.
Then he took out all the markers.
"Lucky for me, my mom is out," he said.

Arnie started to get nervous. "I'd better hide
these for a while," he thought.

Arnie was a nervous wreck. "I'd better go
outside. Harvey may come looking for me,"
he said.

It was late in the afternoon when Arnie got home. He nearly fainted when he got to his room.

His mom had made his bed, and the markers
were sitting right on top!!!

"Where did those come from?" asked
Arnie's mom.
Arnie was going to lie, but it was no use.
"I took them from Harvey's!" he cried.

"I want you to go to Harvey's right now and
tell him you stole these markers. You've
opened them, so you'll have to pay him back!"
yelled Mom. She was *real* mad!

Arnie dreaded telling Harvey he'd stolen
the markers. "I'll probably be sent to jail,"
he thought.

Arnie went in and confessed to Harvey that he had stolen the markers. "Please don't send me to jail," he cried.

"Well, you can work off the price of the markers at the store, every day after school. You can start now. Here's a mop. Get to work," said Harvey.

All week long, Arnie went to Harvey's after school. He worked very hard.

But sometimes it was fun to work at Harvey's.
His friend George thought it was neat that
Arnie had a real job!

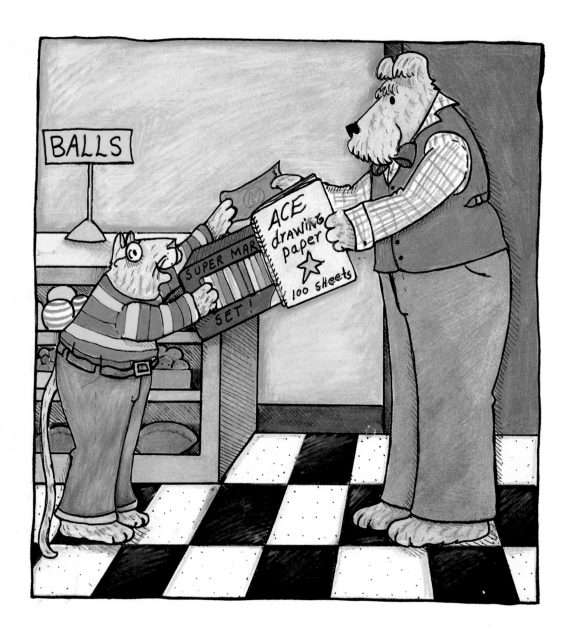

By Saturday Arnie had earned enough to pay
Harvey for the markers.
"You are a good worker," said Harvey. He even
gave Arnie some paper to draw pictures on!

Arnie had no money left for candy. He was just leaving, when Louanne asked him if he'd like to play catch.

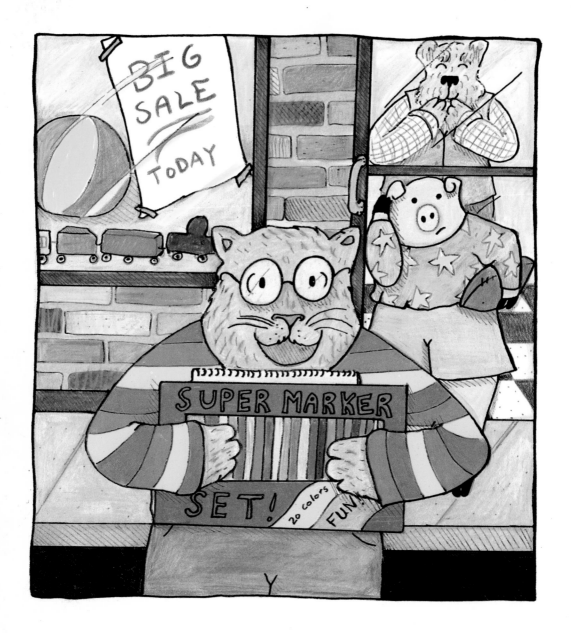

"No," said Arnie. "I think I'll go home and
color with my markers. I've earned it!!!"